Jellybean

EVE AINSWORTH

ILLUSTRATED BY
THEO PARISH

Barrington Stoke

Published by Barrington Stoke
An imprint of HarperCollins*Publishers*
1 Robroyston Gate, Glasgow, G33 1JN

www.barringtonstoke.co.uk

HarperCollins*Publishers*
Macken House, 39/40 Mayor Street Upper,
Dublin 1, DO1 C9W8, Ireland

First published in 2025

ISBN 978-0-00-873952-2

10 9 8 7 6 5 4 3 2 1

A catalogue record for this book is available from the British Library

Printed and bound in India by Replika Press Pvt. Ltd.

This book contains FSC™ certified paper and other controlled sources to ensure responsible forest management.

For more information visit: www.harpercollins.co.uk/green

To anyone who has ever struggled with anxiety.
You are not alone x

CHAPTER 1

Ellie Bean is walking. It's a walk she knows well. She knows she has to go along the street outside her house down to the end and then turn right onto the main road.

There's a lot of traffic on the main road. It's loud at this time of the morning, and Ellie has to use the lights to cross over. Then it's three more roads, one more set of lights and a short trip down the path that runs past the shops.

And then she will be there.

She will be at school.

Ellie takes a deep breath. Her bag isn't that heavy, but it's uncomfy. She's not used to carrying it any more.

Her new school shoes feel stiff and tight, and they hit the ground hard as she walks. Her coat is a little too big, and she is already feeling hot in the soft morning light.

It will only take a few more minutes and she will be there. It's not a big deal. All she has to do is keep moving.

But Ellie feels like she is moving through thick mud. Her legs don't seem to want to take her in the right direction, and her head is full of thoughts and questions.

Because Ellie is terrified.

This isn't a normal day for her.

In fact, it's one of the scariest of her life.

*

Ellie's mum had done her best to keep Ellie calm before she left the house this morning. She had made Ellie's very favourite breakfast (pancakes with maple syrup) and played her favourite music to help her relax.

"It's just another day," her mum said. "Your friends will be there. Holly, Sophie and Meg can't wait to see you."

Ellie had nodded. She wanted to see them too. They had sent her messages last night. They called her by her nickname "Jellybean" and made her laugh with silly jokes. They had made lots of plans. They were going to meet up every break and lunchtime. Holly was going to walk with Ellie to lessons. Ellie wasn't ever going to be by herself.

"You're doing your favourite things today too," her mum added. "Art, History and double English."

These were the lessons that Ellie had missed the most. She loved English, and part of her couldn't wait to get back to the class.

And yet it had been so difficult to finish her breakfast, to chew her pancakes and to tell her mum that she was going to be OK.

It felt like a lie.

*

Ellie is closer to school. Every breath, every step is taking her nearer. At the end of the road, she sees other pupils in the same uniform as her. They are in small groups, laughing and joking as they walk to school.

Ellie feels as if there is a dark cloud inside her.

This is the first time she has done this journey in so long because Ellie hasn't been to school for nearly a year.

CHAPTER 2

Ellie can't tell anyone why school is hard. This isn't because it's a big secret or she is too scared to tell anyone. It's because she can't explain.

It feels impossible.

One morning, six months ago, Ellie woke up and felt like she couldn't move. She had been feeling worried about school for a while, but this time, on this morning, it felt worse than ever before. She looked across her bedroom at her school uniform and felt sick. How was she going to get up? How was she going to get ready? She felt terrified.

When her mum came to hurry her up, Ellie told her she couldn't go to school that day.

"Are you ill?" her mum asked.

"I just – I just can't go today ..."

Ellie began to shake, and seconds later she started to cry.

Her parents let her stay at home. They thought she would feel better by the next day, but she didn't. She woke up with the exact same feelings.

"I can't do it," she sobbed. "It's like my body won't work properly. It feels too heavy and slow."

Her mum tried to get her to put her uniform on, but it made Ellie shake even more. She had to run to the toilet to be sick.

"Has anything happened?" her mum asked.

Ellie tried to think. The truth was she had been anxious about school for some time. At first, it had just been the worry about getting things right – finding the right classroom, handing in her homework, making new friends.

But then other things began to worry her. The corridors were too loud and busy. She didn't like how noisy the lunch hall was, and she was often too shy to order the food she wanted. And then, yesterday, a

301

teacher had shouted at her for daydreaming in class. It was so different from her small primary school.

Ellie told her mum she didn't know what was wrong. It was silly to be scared, she thought.

She just hoped she would feel better tomorrow.

The problem was she didn't.

"Has something happened to make you scared?" her dad asked gently the next day. "Has someone been mean to you? Or said something?"

Ellie shook her head. She had good friends – it wasn't that. No one had been mean.

"Are the lessons too hard? Is it difficult to keep up?" her mum asked.

Ellie shook her head again. She liked learning. She was in the top set for most of her subjects. She hoped to train to be a vet one day. She felt worried that she wasn't at school. Would she fall behind?

"What is it then? How can we help you?" they both asked.

Ellie thought again of the busy school corridors, the loud noise of the other children and all the things that she had to remember and do. It felt as if there was a dark swirling cloud inside of her, making her feel ill.

"It's just school itself," she said. "It scares me now."

Because that was the truth.

CHAPTER 3

The days passed into a week.

And then another.

Ellie still wasn't going to school.

She had heard her mum and dad arguing about it when they thought she couldn't hear them.

Her mum thought that Ellie just needed to get up and get back to school. That she was trying to get attention. She heard her mum complain that she still had to work and couldn't look after Ellie all day long. This made Ellie feel bad.

But her dad seemed to understand that there was more going on – that Ellie was really unhappy and that they couldn't force her to go to school until she was ready.

Her parents took her to see their doctor – Dr Morgan. Ellie had only met her a few times before – once when she had had a bad throat and another time when her ear had been really sore. It was difficult to explain to

Dr Morgan how she was feeling. It wasn't like having a pain that she could point out.

"Does the thought of school make you feel anxious?" Dr Morgan asked.

Ellie thought of the dark cloud and nodded.

"Can you remember what started it?" the doctor asked.

"Not really," Ellie whispered. "It's lots of things, and now just thinking of going to school makes me feel horrible and I want to be sick."

"Are the school helping you?" her doctor asked.

"They are keen for Ellie to come back, but they understand she is struggling," her mum said. "They have been sending work home for her, and we have a meeting with an Education Welfare Officer tomorrow."

Ellie stared around the small room – at the paintings on the wall of pretty seaside places and the photo on the doctor's desk of a girl laughing. She looked the same age as Ellie. Perhaps she was the doctor's daughter. Ellie wished she could feel happy like that again.

"We can refer you to CAMHS," Dr Morgan said. "That's Child and Adolescent Mental Health Services. They can help with feelings like this. There may be a bit of a wait, but it would be good to refer you quickly."

Her mum patted Ellie's leg. "We just want to help you, Ellie."

"I also think that you should see a counsellor. There's a good private service I can put you in touch with," Dr Morgan said, and handed a leaflet to Ellie. "All the details are in here. Meanwhile, you need to look after yourself – eat well, sleep, exercise and get plenty of fresh air. All of these things will help."

Ellie took the leaflet and tried hard not to crush it. It all sounded a bit scary, but she didn't want to look like a baby. She felt nervous, but she made herself smile.

*

The lady from school visited the next day. Her name was Jo Glover, and she told Ellie she was an Education Welfare Officer.

"I'm going to help you as much as I can," she said. "Can you tell me what's been going on?"

Jo had a nice, kind face and sat and listened to Ellie as she tried to explain how she was feeling. Jo also asked about her friends.

"I have three close friends," Ellie told her. "Holly, Sophie and Meg. Holly is my oldest friend. I've known her since playschool."

"You must miss them?" said Jo.

"I do," Ellie nodded.

Holly and Meg had come over to visit at the weekend, which was nice, but when they talked about school, Ellie had the same scary thoughts.

The thoughts were so big and scary that Ellie thought it would be better not to see her friends. It had made her sad to see Holly and Meg and remember what she was missing.

"Your mum tells me they call you Jellybean," Jo said, laughing. "That's a cool nickname."

"It's also my favourite sweet," Ellie grinned.

Jo nudged her with her arm. “Mine too. We might have more in common than you think.”

Ellie smiled and felt herself relax a little bit.

Jo explained that school would continue to send work home for now, but she wanted to get Ellie back into school as soon as possible.

"In the meantime, I want you to have a think about the things that might help you," Jo said. "Keep to a routine at home with your work, and be happy and proud about the little steps that you make."

"Do you think I will be able to go back to school?" Ellie asked.

Jo nodded. "I'm sure you will. We just need to help you with those anxious thoughts you're having." She smiled. "And stay in touch with your friends – that's important. It's good to know you have people who care about you."

Ellie smiled back. Jo was right about that.

CHAPTER 4

Ellie worked hard to be relaxed and happy the next time her friends visited a week later. All three were coming this time – even Sophie, who lived out of town.

Ellie's mum had ordered them pizza, and they were going to watch a movie together.

Holly gave her a big hug as soon as she arrived. "I'm missing you so much, Jellybean," she said. “Maths is rubbish now that I don’t have you to sit with.”

“Poor Holly has to sit with Jasmine,” Meg joked. “You know how boring she is.”

Ellie smiled, but inside she felt sad. So Jasmine had taken her place next to Holly. Ellie knew that Jasmine wasn’t boring at all. Meg had said that to make her feel better.

“Do you think you’ll be coming back soon?” Sophie asked softly.

Ellie shook her head. “I’m not sure. I want to, but at the moment I don’t feel ready.”

Holly gave her arm a squeeze. "Hopefully it won't be long before you are."

Ellie smiled, feeling the tears spring up in her eyes. She missed her friends so much.

As they ate pizza, the girls told Ellie all the things that were happening at school.

"We have a new English teacher, Mr Norris," Sophie told her. "He's so nice – he even gives out prizes at the end of the week for the best writer."

"Yeah, and the canteen food is loads better. A new company has taken over. Everything doesn't taste like feet now," Holly said.

Ellie laughed at this. The food had been something that everyone moaned about. It was good it had improved.

“We hang around with Alice Mockler and Chloe Jennings at lunch now,” Meg said. “They are really funny.”

Ellie looked up, surprised. “I thought you always said they were mean girls?”

Meg gave a shrug. “Turns out they’re not. Not really. They just like having a laugh.”

Ellie tried to ignore the heavy feeling that was filling her up. She put down the rest of her pizza and pushed it away. She couldn’t face eating any more.

Everything was changing so fast, and she had no way of making it stop.

*

A week later, Ellie messaged her friends again, asking if they would like to come over for a sleepover.

Meg answered almost straight away: *Sorry, Jellybean. We're going out with Alice on Friday. Maybe another time?*

Ellie nodded sadly. Maybe.

Holly sent a reply too: *When you're back, I'm sure we can all hang out together. Alice is really funny.*

Ellie didn't reply to that. She didn't know what to say. She felt like she was getting left behind.

She lay on her bed and tucked her phone away under her pillow so she couldn't see it.

All she wanted to feel was normal. She wanted to be with her friends, doing all the stuff that she used to do, but instead this dark, scary cloud stopped her.

Would things ever be OK again?

CHAPTER 5

Two months had passed, and it was nearly Christmas. Ellie was in a new kind of normal now. She didn't enjoy missing school, but she had got used to the routine of being at home; the thought of changing the routine was totally terrifying.

Jo, the Education Welfare Officer, visited often. She would talk to Ellie about school and the different ways she could return.

Maybe Ellie could look at a reduced timetable so she'd go in for fewer days to begin with until she was used to school again.

Her parents thought that was a good idea, and Ellie said she'd like to try it.

"Not yet though," she said.

Her parents didn't say anything, but Ellie knew they were sad she didn't want to go back to school yet. Her mum was doing her admin job from home, but she wouldn't be able to do that for ever.

Ellie was anxious she was making problems for her family because she was staying at home and not going to school.

She told Jo that she really wanted to go back, but the thought of school still made her feel sick and her mum had had to put her uniform away somewhere Ellie didn't have to look at it.

Jo smiled at her kindly. "Don't worry. We'll find something that works for you," she said. "The most important thing is that we go at your pace."

School was still sending work home, but Ellie knew that she was falling behind.

At the moment, she was reading a book for English and following some online classes for Maths. Maths was difficult, and she wished she had a teacher to explain it to her. Her mum tried to help, but it wasn't the same.

Jo asked what sort of things Ellie liked to do outside of school. Ellie told her she loved art, so Jo told her to try to do some at home.

"Maybe drawing and painting will help with your feelings," she said. "And it might help you relax."

Mum brought home some new paint and pencils from the shops, and Ellie would sit and draw in the kitchen after she had done some

of her schoolwork. It felt good to be doing the things she liked again. She designed and made Christmas cards for her friends.

"Jo was telling me about some home-education support groups," Mum told her later. "These are groups for children who don't go to school for all sorts of reasons, and they meet up in person sometimes. It might be something we could do?"

Ellie nodded, but she wasn't sure. It wasn't that she didn't want to go to school, she just couldn't at the moment.

She wished she could explain why school felt so hard.

CHAPTER 6

Christmas came and went. Ellie enjoyed the time with her family and the fact she had more time to see her friends. They asked her if she might come back to school after the holidays, but that made her clam up immediately. She knew she wasn't ready yet.

Instead, she agreed to go to a support group with her mum. The group was small and friendly, with ten children of different ages. Some were home educated, and some were school refusers. Ellie sat next to a boy called Stephen, who was a few years older than her. He showed her some of the coding he was doing on his computer. He was very good at it.

"Why don't you go to school?" she asked.

"I have autism and ADHD," he told her. "I've always struggled with school, even when I was little. Now my mum home-schools me."

Ellie nodded. He seemed happy, but she wasn't sure that was what she wanted to do. Not in the long term anyway.

"I can't go to school at the moment, but I hope to soon," she said quietly.

Stephen grinned at her. "I'm sure you will when you're ready. Sometimes these things just take time."

Ellie smiled back. She hoped he was right.

*

A few weeks later, Ellie woke up from a dream. In it, she had been back at school. Everything had been like before – her friends were with her, and she was having a laugh and going to lessons. It felt natural and normal, like she had never been away.

When Ellie woke up, she realised she was crying. She wished the dream had been true.

She knew with every day that passed it would get harder and harder to go back to school.

Ellie worried that if she went back now, she would find that everyone else had moved on and that everything was different. Would her teachers even remember her? And would her friends have time for her now that they were busy with other people like Alice and Chloe?

It wouldn't be like her dream. She wouldn't fit in any more.

Ellie lay in her bed for a few minutes looking at her messages. Her last one from Sophie yesterday was really sweet:

Hey Jellybean,

We miss you. Mr Jennings is a nightmare in History these days, and I still can't stand Maths.

Joey and Jenna Smith are going out.

Lots of us are going into town after school tomorrow.

Maybe you could come too if you feel up to it?

Ellie answered her now. She told Sophie that she was busy today.

This was kind of true, as she had schoolwork to do, but also she couldn't face going into town and seeing everyone. They would all have questions that she wouldn't be able to answer, and they would probably think she was weird or stupid for not going to school.

Sometimes it was easier to lock yourself away from the rest of the world.

*

After doing some of her schoolwork, Ellie spent the afternoon painting in the kitchen, watching the winter scenes in the garden.

She wasn't really thinking about what she was doing, but instead she just enjoyed putting paint on the paper. It was only when her mum walked over to the table that Ellie looked at what she was painting.

"That's interesting, Ellie. What is it?" Mum asked.

Ellie stared at her picture. She had painted a face – her own face – and around it she had drawn strokes of grey, swirly clouds.

"Is that how you're feeling?" her mum asked gently.

"Yes, I think so," Ellie said.

She thought for a moment.

"There's always too much going on in my head," she went on, "and it feels as if I'm stuck in some kind of fog. It's confusing."

Her mum touched the picture for a moment. "That must be hard," she said softly.

Ellie was still staring at the face she had drawn. She hadn't meant to paint herself like that, and she felt surprised. The face looked sad.

Did Ellie feel sad? Or did she feel scared?

She waited until her mum had walked away, and then she covered up the painting with dark black strokes.

She didn't want to see that face again.

CHAPTER 7

Time passed quickly. It was now February, and one day Ellie woke up because she heard her parents arguing. That didn't happen often, and it made her feel scared. She got out of bed and crept towards her door.

Downstairs, her parents were talking loudly in the living room. It sounded like her mum was very upset.

“She can’t carry on like this for much longer. She’s missing out on too much,” her mum said. “And I need to go back to the office soon, but I don’t like leaving her like this.”

“I know.” Ellie’s dad voice was a little calmer. “But we can’t force her to do anything. We just have to wait until she is ready.”

“But she won’t even tell us what’s really wrong. Maybe she’s too scared to tell us that she’s being bullied?”

Ellie crept back into her bed and pulled the covers over her head.

Why couldn't her parents understand that she just couldn't explain how she was feeling?

She wished she knew what had happened to make her like this. She wished she could tell her parents what the problem was. It was difficult because the longer she was off school, the harder it was to think about going back.

She wished she could be back to how she was before.

*

Later, Mum sat next to her and showed her a website on her phone.

"I know we've been waiting a long time for an appointment with CAMHS," she said. "So your dad and I think you should see a therapist that we pay for, like the one Dr Morgan talked about. Someone told us this therapist was good. She looks very nice," she went on. "I think you should meet with her. Is that OK?"

"Yes," Ellie nodded. "I want to."

"She said she can come to the house first if that's better, and then, when you feel more comfortable, we can go to her office," her mum said. "We will help you through this, Ellie."

Ellie looked up at her mum's tired face.

"I know, Mum," she said softly, and made herself smile.

She had to believe she would get better.

CHAPTER 8

Ellie's therapist was called Fiona. She had long blonde hair and wore colourful long dresses. She greeted Ellie with a huge smile the first time they met.

Fiona came to Ellie's house for the first meeting. Ellie's mum was there too so it wasn't too scary.

Fiona asked Ellie lots of questions about what she liked doing and what she would like to do in the future. When she heard that Ellie was interested in art, Fiona asked to see her paintings.

"These are so good," she said after Ellie had shown her a few. Ellie had done some more paintings of her face, but she had done others of the garden with all the things that made her feel happy, like birds and flowers.

"Really?" Ellie wasn't sure that Fiona was telling the truth.

"Really! I can see you have a lot of talent and also that you're getting a lot of your feelings out here. That's so important," Fiona told her. "Feelings and anxiety can feel scary when they're trapped inside, so it's good to be able to paint them and think about them."

Ellie stared at her pictures for a while. It had felt good to make the paintings, and she always felt calmer after. Maybe Fiona was right.

*

Fiona came to visit Ellie a few more times, and soon Ellie felt comfortable about going to see her at her office. It was a nice bright space, and it was good to get out of the house. At first, her mum took her in the car, but after a while, Ellie agreed to walk there with her.

The office was only a few streets away from Ellie's school, and although Ellie still felt a tugging feeling inside of her thinking about that, it wasn't as bad as it had been.

Fiona got Ellie to write down the things she was worried about at school one by one, and then they talked about what Ellie could do and who she could talk to when she was feeling like this.

Fiona also taught her to breathe in a special slow way and to think about different helpful things when she was struggling.

Ellie liked doing that. She thought about a place that made her feel safe, like home, and then about the smells, sights and sounds in that place. It helped to calm Ellie a bit and helped her brain tune into something happy.

"I think talking to Fiona is helping," she told her mum. "It feels like there's more space in my head."

The horrible anxious feeling inside was starting to settle. Fiona was giving her things to do if she felt stressed – tools to help her when she felt bad.

"I'm proud of you," her mum said, and gave Ellie's hand a little squeeze.

CHAPTER 9

It was now March, just a few weeks before Easter, and both Ellie and her parents thought this was the right time for her to try school again – that way she would have a short break again if she needed it.

"We don't want to force this on you, Ellie," her mum said.

"Yes – only do it if you're ready," her dad added, smiling.

They were sitting together in the living room. Jo was there too. She had written up a part-time timetable for Ellie. They'd worked it out together and with the school. Ellie was going to try to go back to school but only for a few hours at a time. To begin with, Jo said she could just try a few mornings and come home at lunch.

Ellie looked at the timetable and tried to ignore the flutters inside her tummy.

"I want to try," she said. "I really do want to try to go back to school."

"We can drive you there in the car," her dad said.

"No. Thanks for the offer, but I want to try walking in," Ellie replied. "I used to walk to school, and I want to try to do that again."

Ellie liked walking, and she hoped it would help to clear her head.

She also wanted to see if she could make it past the school gate by herself.

"It doesn't matter if you don't," her mum told her. "Just take it one step at a time."

*

Later that day, Ellie messaged her friends and told them her plans.

Yay! Jellybean! We can't wait to see you! Sophie wrote.

Finally, I can have my friend back in Maths, Meg said.

I can meet you at the gate or walk a bit with you. You're not alone, said Holly.

Ellie blinked away the tears. She was so lucky to have such good friends. They hadn't forgotten her. She hoped she would see them in school very soon.

CHAPTER 10

So now Ellie is walking. It's a walk she knows well. She knows she has to go along the street outside her house down to the end and then turn right onto the main road.

There's a lot of traffic on the main road. It's loud at this time of the morning, and Ellie has to use the lights to cross over. Then it's three more roads, one more set of lights and a short trip down the path that runs past the shops.

And then she will be there.

She will be at school.

She keeps walking.

As the school gets closer, she can see the crowds of other pupils in little groups chatting before the bell goes. Ellie's heart beats a little faster.

The noise gets louder now, and Ellie remembers how bad she felt before. Her body starts to shake again. She starts to feel sick.

She can't be sick. Not now. She thinks of her home, of how safe it is there, and tries to remember those feelings and use them to help her calm down now. She tries to control her breathing like Fiona taught her.

In.

Out.

In.

Out.

The school is only a road away. She can see the gate from here.

She stops.

She has a decision to make. Does she carry on walking into school?

Or does she go back home?

She closes her eyes, takes another deep breath and then she chooses.

Further Information

For Parents/Carers

What is Emotionally Based School Avoidance (EBSA) or school refusal?

There can be lots of reasons for children and young people to feel anxious about going to school, such as the pressure of schoolwork, falling out with friends or feeling overwhelmed in the school environment. Sometimes an external issue like an illness in the family or the responsibility of being a young carer can make it difficult to feel settled in school.

If these feelings build up to the point where someone can't face going to school, the child or young person is often labelled as a "school refuser", but this makes it sound as if they are simply choosing not to go to school, so it is better to use the terms Emotionally Based School Avoidance (EBSA) or Anxiety-Related Absence.

Some parents also choose to home educate their children because they feel that their needs are not being met at school, but this is different to school avoidance.

What might Emotionally Based School Avoidance look like?

It's very common for young people to feel anxious now and again, but some can have ongoing and heightened feelings of anxiety related to school that can cause long-term problems. If this is the case, they might:

- not want to get up in the morning and get ready for school;
- become upset when it's time to leave for school;
- experience physical symptoms like headaches, tummy aches or feeling sick;
- have difficulty sleeping;
- struggle to complete schoolwork or homework;
- avoid school altogether.

For Children/Young People

Who can help?

It's important to speak to someone as soon as you start to feel anxious about school. This could be your parents or carers, and your class teacher could help you to find out what support is available in school, such as a safe space or time-out card you could use when feeling anxious. Educational Welfare Officers can also work with you to identify strategies to help you at school.

If you are really struggling, your GP might refer you to CAMHS (Child and Adolescent Mental Health Services) for further support.

Tips to help day to day

- Practising mindfulness can be useful. Mindfulness means paying attention to the moment you are in and noticing your emotions, thoughts and feelings, and accepting them instead of reacting to them. There are lots of different exercises you can do, such as counting your breaths, and you can find more information here:

bbcchildreninneed.co.uk/schools/primary-school/mindfulness-hub

youngminds.org.uk/professional/resources/mindfulness-activities

- Try writing down any worries and sharing them with your family and teachers. This can be easier than talking about them, and writing down worries gets them out of your head.

- Do things that help you relax after school. This could be listening to music, spending time with your friends or playing a sport.

- Recognise your small achievements. Getting out of bed on time, completing your homework and being on time for school are all big wins.

- Don't be upset when you have a bad day. Everyone's moods go up and down. This is natural. Be kind to yourself.

Further help and support

youngminds.org.uk

schoolavoidance.org

parentkind.org.uk

ipsea.org.uk

Our books are tested
for children and young people by
children and young people.

Thanks to everyone who consulted on
a manuscript for their time and effort in
helping us to make our books better
for our readers.